HENRY

3

JAMES

5

PERCY

6

MEET ALL THESE FRIENDS IN BUZZ BOOKS:

Thomas the Tank Engine
The Wind in the Willows
Skeleton Warriors
Fireman Sam
In My Pocket

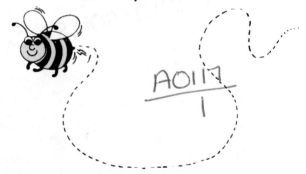

First published in Great Britain 1996
by Buzz Books
an imprint of Reed Children's Books
Michelin House, 81 Fulham Road, London SW3 6RB
and Auckland, Melbourne, Singapore and Toronto

Copyright © 1996 William Heinemann Ltd
All publishing rights: William Heinemann Ltd. All television and
merchandising rights licensed by William Heinemann Ltd
to Britt Allcroft (Thomas) Ltd exclusively, worldwide.
Photographs copyright © 1995 Britt Allcroft (Thomas) Ltd
Photographs by David Mitton and Terry Permane for Britt Allcroft's
production of *Thomas the Tank Engine and Friends*

ISBN 1 85591 557 X

Printed in Italy by Olivotto

BULLDOG

buzz books

One morning, Percy was impatient. The other engines were still dozing but not Percy.

"Driver should be here by now. What's he doing!?"

"Sleeping," grunted Gordon.

"But that means I'll be late, the coaches will be waiting and the passengers will get cross," moaned Percy.

"Never mind Percy," said Thomas. "It'll soon be time for work but be careful or you might run into danger. And," he added, "Duke is not here to save you."

"Duke," stuttered Toby. "You mean our hero?"

"The very same," said Thomas. "Driver told me the whole story..."

And this is the story Thomas told them...

Long ago when Peter Sam was called Stuart and Sir Handel was known as Falcon, they worked with Duke on the old railway. But Falcon still had a lot to learn.

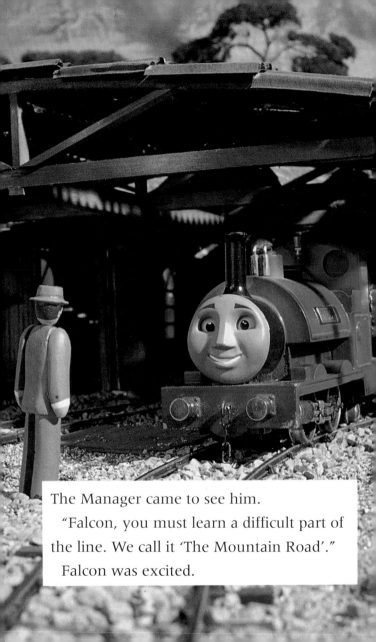

The Manager came to see him.

"Falcon, you must learn a difficult part of the line. We call it 'The Mountain Road'."

Falcon was excited.

"So tomorrow," continued the Manager, "when you have a new coat of paint, you will go on it. Duke will explain everything."

"Huh!" thought Falcon. "Duke's just a fusspot."

Next day came.

"Listen," warned Duke. "The Mountain Road is difficult. I'll lead."

"No," replied Falcon. "Driver says I'll lead. How can I learn the route with you blocking the view?"

"Suit yourself," said Duke, "but never mind the view. Look at the track."

The engines set off on their journey at once. They steamed over the river bridge and started the long, steep climb up into the mountains.

The engines' speed grew slower and slower and slower.

"Don't dawdle, don't dawdle," urged Falcon, impatiently.

"No hurry, no hurry," puffed Duke.

Quite soon, they approached a tunnel.
But Falcon didn't like the tunnel.
   "I want to get out," he sighed to himself.
Presently they came to the other side.

"Watch the track, watch the track," warned Duke.

One moment everything seemed safe, but then suddenly...

Falcon was derailed with one wheel dangerously near the edge. Duke bravely held on with all his strength.

"Stop shaking," called Duke. "I can't hold you if you shake."

Falcon tried hard to stop shuddering.

Duke's Driver and Fireman worked
quickly to make the two engines safe again.
Then came more trouble.

"Water," cried Duke's Fireman. "Duke needs water quickly."

Luckily there was a workman's cottage nearby. Soon, everyone was passing jugs, buckets and saucepans filled with water until Duke's thirst was quenched.

As Duke's steam pressure gradually started to rise, he began to feel stronger and stronger.

At last, with everyone's help, he was able to pull Falcon back on the rails. Then they started off once more.

The Manager was waiting at the Top
Station.

"Your Duke," said the passengers, "is a hero. He stood firm like a bulldog and wouldn't let go."

Falcon was grateful too.

"Thank you for saving me Duke. I don't know why you bothered with me after I'd been so rude."

"Oh well," Duke replied, "you'd just had
a new coat of paint. It would have been a
pity if you'd rolled down the mountain
and spoilt it!"

THOMAS

EDWARD

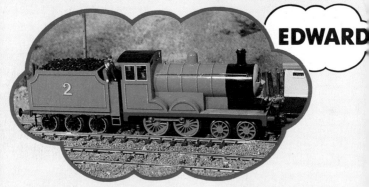

GORDON